A catalogue record for this book is available from the British Library

Published by Ladybird Books Ltd
27 Wrights Lane London W8 5TZ
A Penguin Company

4 6 8 10 9 7 5 3

LADYBIRD and the device of a Ladybird are trademarks of Ladybird Books Ltd

Printed in Italy

Disney's

DINOSAUR

Ladybird

Once, millions of years ago, a dinosaur egg dropped out of the sky onto Lemur Island.

The egg had been on an amazing journey. First a hungry lizard had stolen it from a nest. But then the egg dropped into a river where a bird found it.

The bird flew the egg across the ocean where it landed in a tree and cracked open to reveal a baby dinosaur... right in front of a family of lemurs!

The lemurs, Plio, Yar and Zini, took care of the little dinosaur and named him Aladar. They watched him grow from a tiny baby into a giant, but gentle, Iguanodon.

Once every year Aladar went with the lemurs to a special meeting place where they chose their mates. Everyone was happy, except Plio, who was sad. She knew that Aladar would never find a mate of his own on the island.

One night an enormous fireball crashed into the sea and a giant wave of fire headed towards the island.

Aladar raced to the cliffs, with the lemurs clinging to his neck. He could barely keep ahead of the flames. At the last moment he leapt into the sea and swam to the mainland.

Safe on the shore, Aladar and the lemurs looked back at their home. It had been completely destroyed.

Suddenly the ground beneath them began to rumble. A herd of huge creatures stomped through the dust towards them.

"They're just like me!" thought Aladar.

So Aladar and the lemurs joined the herd. Soon they became good friends with two old dinosaurs, Baylene and Eema.

Baylene explained that the herd was heading for the Nesting Grounds.

As Aladar walked with them, he grew worried about his two new dinosaur friends. The fireball had dried up most of the land and there was no food or water. Baylene and Eema were also very tired. So Aladar decided to speak to Kron, the leader of the herd.

"Maybe you could slow down a bit?" suggested Aladar.

"Watch yourself, boy!" Kron warned. He didn't care about the weaker ones. And he thought Aladar wanted to take his place as leader.

At last the herd reached a dried up lakebed. Baylene's heavy feet squashed and squished as she plodded wearily on through the sand.

"Baylene, press down!" cried Aladar. Her deep footprint filled with water from underground.

"Water!" Aladar cried to the rest of the herd. The dinosaurs went wild and pushed and shoved for a place to get a drink. Aladar protected his friends.

Later that evening, Neera, Kron's sister, stood beside Aladar at the waterhole.

"Why did you help those old ones?" she asked him.

"If we look out for each other, we will all stand a better chance of getting to your Nesting Grounds," Aladar answered.

Neera was amazed. She had never met another dinosaur who cared as much for others as Aladar did.

And Aladar had never met another dinosaur that he liked as much as Neera! He knew they would always be friends.

Next day, Kron ordered the herd to move on at double speed. Bruton, one of the dinosaurs who went ahead of the herd to look out for danger, had returned and he was badly injured. He had been attacked by a fierce, meat-eating Carnotaur.

Aladar knew that the older ones would not be able to keep up with the herd. And he chose to stay behind to help them. So he sadly said goodbye to Neera.

Not long afterwards, Aladar and his
friends found Bruton. Bruton had also
stayed behind, to look for the Carnotaurs,
but his wounds were very bad. Aladar
took him into a cave to shelter.

Suddenly some hungry Carnotaurs came into the cave.

Bruton bravely fought the Carnotaurs but he was injured again, and when Aladar went to help him, it was too late.

Aladar returned sadly to his friends. Zini had found a way out at the back of the cave but it was blocked by some rocks. "We're not meant to survive!" sighed Aladar.

"Shame on you!" said Baylene. "I, for one, am getting out of here!"

So, encouraged, the friends didn't stop digging until…

...they stepped out into the fresh air and the green valley of the Nesting Grounds.

"It's really beautiful!" said Aladar. "But where's the rest of the herd?"

"Look," said Eema sadly, "a huge landslide has blocked the entrance. They'll never get through."

Aladar decided to set out alone to save Neera and the rest of the herd. When he found them he cried out, "Follow me! I know a safer way."

But Kron was furious and jealous of Aladar. "They're staying with me!" he growled and he knocked Aladar down.

Neera rushed to his rescue whilst Kron stood alone on the rocks. Suddenly a hungry Carnotaur attacked the herd.

"Stand together!" cried Aladar and he started to bellow. The rest of the herd did the same.

So the Carnotaur attacked Kron instead. Kron was badly wounded. Neera and Aladar knew he wouldn't make it.

Safe, but saddened,
Aladar and Neera nuzzled
each other. The herd
roared their
thanks, and then
finished
their
journey.
***
Several weeks
later, Aladar
stood beside
Neera.

One of the eggs in their nest cracked open in front of them, and out crawled a beautiful baby dinosaur.

"Oh, happy, happy day!" cried Eema, and all the friends agreed.